Narra & Boccy Adventures

Not another zebra

Story and illustrations
by Graham James

Narra and Boccy are relaxing in a park away from the **noisy** city,

taking pictures of all the wild life around them.

SNAP SNAP goes Narra's camera.

Narra uploads the pictures to their blog to share with their family and friends.

Boccy points to a message on Narra's home page.

Honk!
Honk! H

LOOKING for an adventure?
Enter one of the **hardest** competitions in the world.
Click here for more details. CLICK!

TRY AND FIND THE BIG FIVE

WIN

WIN

Rhino, Buffalo, Elephant, Lion and not forgetting the LEOPARD.

ARE YOU UP FOR IT?

By the way, the Leopard is the shyest of the Big Five and will be a challenge to find.

"Boccy! Just think of the pictures we could take and share" Narra said excitedly.

Narra and Boccy booked their flights
and set out for the airport.

During the flight they wondered who sent
the advert and what the prizes could be.

A new **CAR**, a **bike** or another **holiday**?

Who knows?

Both agreed it was going to be hard to get all five, especially the leopard.

Narra and Boccy were so excited to start searching for the BIG FIVE.

After driving around for hours and hours in the hot **SUN**,

Narra and Boccy started to feel **SAD** as they hadn't seen a single animal.

"DON'T worry we will have better **LUCK**

tomorrow" the driver said.

The next day, **SUCCess!**

zebras were everywhere.

"Look over there." The driver whispered.

"Where? Which way?" Narra and Boccy whispered back.

"There, in the distance, two giant Giraffes!"
the driver said happily.

Another picture for the collection! But none of these animals are part of the Big Five.

Look!

Rhinos

relaxing in the afternoon sun!

Narra and Boccy get their first animal from the Big Five. Four more animals to go!

Wow!

A Lion sleeping under a tree!

Shhhhhhhhh!

Let's be as quiet as possible.

Can you see the leopard in that tree?

The next day, Narra and Boccy get up bright

and **early** to go up in a hot air balloon

to find some elephants.

Two more animals to go! I think that zebra is following Narra and Boccy.

eeeeerrrrrrr

The driver slams on the brakes
as hard as he could as a herd of
Buffalo cross in front of the car.

It must have been Narra and Boccy's lucky day;

there's another leopard over there on the rocks!

Narra and Boccy couldn't believe it; that zebra had **photo bombed** ANOTHER picture.

It was Narra and Boccy's last day and still no picture of a Leopard.

The zebra could see that Narra and Boccy were sad and wanted

to help them find a Leopard to complete all the photos of the Big Five.

Inside a cave, a family of leopards were laughing. Ha Ha Ha Ha Ha Ha Ha

They had been hiding from Narra and Boccy while they were trying to take photos.

But instead the leopards were taking photos of Narra and Boccy for their own collection.

"FOUND YOU!" Shouted Narra and Boccy.

"Then who was it?"

The zebra looked at Narra and Bocoy and told them,

"It was me. I'm sorry. I wanted to make some new friends and have an adventure."

Narra and Boccy didn't mind as they had the best adventure ever.

Look at all these animals

Rhinos, Buffalos, Giraffes, Elephants, Lions, Monkeys, Impalas and not forgetting the Leopards and their new friend the zebra.

This story is based on one of the adventures that Graham and
his wife (Diane) had before their son Eli was born.
Eli does not believe them; because he thinks
Mummy and Daddy don't do anything fun, Little does he know.

ISBN-978-0-473-41639-3 (Softcover)   ISBN-978-0-473-41640-9 (Hardcover)
ISBN-978-0-473-41641-6 (ePub)   ISBN-978-0-473-41642-3(mobi)

www.pupgon.com

Published by 'PupGon' Publishing, New Zealand

Made in the USA
San Bernardino, CA
18 November 2017